ROME for the

JUDY AN...

BILLIONAIRE HOLIDAY SERIES
Book 1

Rome for the Holidays

The BILLIONAIRE HOLIDAY Series, Volume 1

JUDY ANGELO

Published by Judy Angelo, 2014.

ROME FOR THE HOLIDAYS

First edition. February 10, 2014.

Copyright © 2014 JUDY ANGELO.

ISBN: 979-8201901509

Written by JUDY ANGELO.

Rome for the Holidays

TALK ABOUT SEXY AS sin...

Arie Angelis is floored when she lays eyes on the handsome hunk seated at the head table at the holiday event she's catering. She literally can't take her eyes off him. She's always prided herself on being the consummate professional, but not this time. But, attracted or not, when she finds out who he is, she realizes he's way out of her reach. But this is one girl who never let a challenge stop her.

Rome Milano is used to getting what he wants, but when he meets the hot and heavenly Arie Angelis, he soon learns that he can't always have his way. He's used to calling the shots, but with this little lady, not this time!

CHAPTER ONE

"Arie Angelis. get over here. Stop staring at that man."

Arie ignored Lena's fierce whisper. Her business partner didn't know a good thing when she saw it. "Are you kidding me?" she whispered back as she hid in the shadow of the passageway. "Look at him."

From her hiding place, she drank her fill of tanned skin, chiseled jaw and lips that were dying to be kissed. Mercy, had God given him those lips to torture women the world over? She couldn't tear her eyes away from them.

And then, those eyes – deep, dark, liquid brown – they gleamed in the light cast by the candles on his table, now making him look so intense, and then giving him a look so sultry that her heart literally picked up pace. A smile curled Arie's lips. If the man only knew the effect he was having on an unknown woman hiding in the shadows, a total stranger to him.. But, then again, maybe he did. He probably had that effect on every woman within viewing distance of him...and he knew it. She could see it in the way he sat, back straight, confidence exuding from him as he surveyed the room. And it didn't help that his raven-dark hair curled sexily just above the collar of his obviously expensive suit. God, he was just too much.

"Aristotle Angelis, if you don't remove yourself this minute -"

"All right, all right, I'm coming." Arie backed away, then turned to give her friend a searing look. "And will you stop reminding me about my joke of a name? You know I hate it."

Lena, her hands filled with table napkins and her face sporting a grin, came a step closer and nodded. "It got your attention, didn't it?" Her smile widened. "Like it always does."

Arie smiled back and shook her head. "My birth mother must have hated me, to saddle me with such a name. She must have been one weird Greek girl."

"Oh, come on. It's a beautiful name. It makes you sound smart, even if you're not." Lena almost burst out laughing when Arie made after her, but then she stifled it and drew closer to the drapes behind which Arie had been hiding. She peered out at the banquet hall full of diners as they ate their meal, some chatting, some laughing, while others focused their attention on the sumptuous spread before them. "Finished checking him out?" she asked.

"No, not yet," Arie said, drawing closer so she could peep out again, "but how can I, when I have you bugging me every second?"

"I'm bugging you," Lena said slowly, almost patiently, "because our team members are wondering why they're busy working while the boss is over here, ogling one of our clients."

Arie rolled her eyes. "Oh, please. I bet they didn't even notice."

Lena chuckled. "Don't be so sure of that. They've been doing some ogling of their own. And not just the girls, either.

Everybody's checking out the celebrity."

That got Arie's attention. "Celebrity? Who is he? An actor? No, he's

3

got to be a model, right?"

"Nope. He's a bigwig in the company. They say he likes to keep a low profile but he's pretty big."

Arie lifted an eyebrow. "Oh, he is, is he?"

Lena nodded. "Yes, he is, so take your eyes off him, sister. He's way out of your league."

Now, if that wasn't a dare, Arie didn't know what was. And if Lena had really wanted her to back off, the last thing she should have done was present her with a challenge like that.

"Oh, yeah?" she mumbled, even as she turned to head back to the kitchen and to her catering staff. "We'll just see about that."

Arie was soon back in 'boss' mode, making sure her team moved with the smooth efficiency that had made Talk of the Town the catering company of choice for corporate and social events all across Louisiana. She and her college roommate had formed the company four years earlier and now, at the age of twenty-seven, she could count herself as one of the successful businesspeople in her community, the classic rags-to-riches story.

She'd been one of the unfortunate ones who hadn't been adopted into a family. Maybe it had been her independent spirit, maybe her unusual name. Who knew? Instead of enjoying the security of one loving family, she'd moved from foster home to foster home, spending two years here, then four years there, until, before she knew it, she was eighteen and off into the big, wild world. Thankfully, she'd been the independent, 'go-getter' type. She'd survived on her own, graduated magna cum laude, and had done darned well for herself, all things considered.

With a savvy friend like Lena Rossini in her life, how could she have gone wrong? Every day she thanked the stars that fate had thrown them together in that tiny dorm room on the Duke campus. That had been the beginning of a partnership that had blossomed into a catering company that benefited from Lena's business acumen and showcased Arie's culinary skills.

And today was more of the same. They'd been contracted by the planning manager of Belitalia to host their sales award dinner, and the fact that the occasion was scheduled just days before Thanksgiving did not faze Arie one bit. Sure, they had six events scheduled over the next four days, but that was what made Talk of the Town so special. When it came to being organized and handling multiple projects efficiently, their reputation was spotless.

But there was just one little problem. Today, for the first time since she'd started her business, Arie was distracted. And it was all the fault of that too, too sexy man sitting at the head table, making her think thoughts that had absolutely nothing to do with cooking or catering.

She shook her head, trying to clear him from her mind, then turned toward her tuxedoed team of well-trained servers, some of them talented apprentice chefs. "Time for the Bananas Foster, guys. Let's get some fires going."

"We're on it, boss." That had to be Paul, always willing, always the first to tackle a task. She smiled as the young man led the way into the massive banquet hall, straight to the specially prepared table in the middle of the room.

There, four of them would prepare the classic New Orleans dessert right there in front of a rapt audience. Of course, with all that fire flaming in the pans, there would always be two other servers watching and waiting in the wings, fire extinguishers in hand. Thankfully, in all her years in the catering business, they'd never had to use that contingency plan.

With the guests totally caught up in the show her team was putting on, Arie saw the perfect opportunity to glide out and, as inconspicuously as possible, make her way from table to table, making sure that all was well. She often did that at big events, just to reduce the likelihood of any eventualities, but today she had an ulterior motive. What better way to get a closer look at the object of her admiration? And no, she wasn't a desperate, sex-starved woman who had nothing better to do with her time. She was just enjoying the view, that was all.

Arie smiled when the staff members of Belitalia burst into applause as Paul finished the dish with a flourish, bowing low in appreciation of their praise. Showman that he was, he was never one to disappoint.

As the chatter and applause died down, she turned, still smiling, and suddenly found herself staring directly into the deep, brown eyes of a man who was watching her so intently that she almost stopped in her tracks. It was her Adonis.

She blinked. That fraction of a second was what it took to unfreeze her and release her from his unwavering stare.

Earlier, she'd been the stalker, but now she knew what it felt like, to be stalked. He was stalking her. Mercy, was he checking her out?

The idea was farfetched, she knew, but contrary or not, it made her nipples pebble in her blouse as she turned and hurried back to the safety of the kitchen.

Lena was laughing as she strode in. "Don't give me that innocent look," she said. "I know what you were up to."

"I was just checking that things were going smoothly."

"Among other things," Lena said, coming this close to rolling her eyes. "Just remember what I said. Out of your league."

Arie only smiled and busied herself with arranging the tea and coffee trays. Lena didn't know it, but her insistence that she back off only made her want to know this guy more. Call it the temptation of the forbidden fruit. Whatever.

All Arie knew was she would not stop until she knew exactly who her mystery man was, and why the heck he'd sparked such a reaction in her. Lena would just have to live with it.

· · ☙ · ·

*B*ELLA. That was the word that came to mind as Rome's eyes locked with the deepest blue ones he'd ever seen. The woman was staring at him with a wide-eyed gaze, a hint of a smile on her lips, a smile that seemed only for him. It was as if they shared a secret from which they'd excluded the rest of world, and that secret was sexy as hell.

As soon as she'd seen him watching her, she'd she dropped her gaze and headed back to the hallway, her long, blonde ponytail bouncing behind her. Within seconds, she'd disappeared into the shadows.

Who the devil was she? She'd stared at him with open candor, a look of admiration in her eyes and a smile on her lips.

She was throwing him an invitation, that much was clear, and he planned to accept. He wouldn't be a man if he didn't.

Wanting to ask about her, he was leaning over to speak to his second-in-command, the chief operating officer of the US division, when he heard his name being called. Damn. Time to head to the podium. As award dinners went, he was expected to give a speech where he would congratulate all the winners and motivate those who had room for improvement. He'd done more than his fair share of these, and he hated them. Public speeches were not his thing, but knowing how important they were, he did them anyway.

To the applause of his employees, he stood and, looking around the room, he gave them a practiced smile. It was one that had served him well in the past, and it would do for tonight, too.

As he approached the front, the clamor rose, and when he climbed the platform and stood behind the podium, he had to hold up a hand to quiet them down. "Welcome, team, and thanks for coming out to support your colleagues as we recognize their efforts and achievements." The applause went up again, with some of the sales reps patting the winners on their backs. "As I promised at our last meeting, because we exceeded the year's sales target, for our next award banquet, the entire team will be flown to the island of Grenada."

That was when the applause got really raucous, with not just hand clapping, but lots of table banging, whoops and cheers. It took a while before Rome could get them quiet enough so he could finish his speech.

As owner and CEO of a successful multinational corporation, he was used to this, not just in the United States, but in his European, Asian and Latin American divisions as well. He was happy when his teams did well, and he was even more so when it was time to reward them for a job well done.

It took another fifteen minutes before he was finally able to return to his seat, handing over to the senior vice president of sales who would hand out the trophies. All the time he'd been on stage, his eyes had been roaming the room in search of the mystery woman who had caught his eye.

And it had been in a big way. He couldn't believe how distracted he'd been on stage, addressing his staff with only one part of his brain, while the rest of him focused on locating the blue-eyed blonde.

And then, he'd found her. Toward the end of his speech, she'd returned to the banquet hall and stood watching him, and this time, she did not drop her gaze, not even when his eyes met hers. He'd locked gazes with her as long as would go unnoticed, but even when he'd turned his attention back to his audience, he was one hundred percent aware of her. There was just something about this woman that he could not shake. And, truth be told, he didn't want to.

Now, freed from the stage and all the attention that came with it, he leaned toward his COO again. "I need some information," he said, his voice low, "on one of the servers."

Tom Billich frowned. "A server? Is there a problem?" He began to look around the room as if searching out the server in question.

"There's no problem. There's just some information I think she may have, information that could prove useful to us." Rome chose his words cautiously. Regardless of his position as CEO – in fact, because of it – he had to tread very carefully, making his interest seem nothing but professional.

Tom's face cleared. "Can you describe her?"

"I can do better than that. Her name tag says 'Arie'. Check her out for me, will you? Get her contact information to my personal assistant and she'll take it from there."

"Consider it done." Tom gave him a brusque nod. "The planning manager made all the arrangements with the catering company. She can get that information to me in quick time."

Rome did not lay eyes on the mysterious Miss Arie again that evening, but by the time he returned to office on Monday, his personal assistant knew exactly how to reach her.

"Have her come in to see me when I get back from Italy," he told her. "Make it a week from Monday."

Iyana looked up from where she'd been tapping on her keyboard. She swiveled her chair around to face him. "Do you have another date I could throw out there? What if she's not available for this one?"

Rome almost laughed. The way that girl had looked at him, he knew she would make herself available.

10

"Just call her," he said, ,as he turned to go back into his office. "I have no doubt she will be."

CHAPTER TWO

With Thanksgiving and all the events that came with it, the past week had been crazy-busy, so busy that she hadn't had time to even boot up her computer. Now that the holiday was behind them, she was finally doing her checks on the man who'd so captivated her from the moment she first laid eyes on him.

"Well, you knew he was big, didn't you? After all, the man was introduced as the CEO." Lena shook her head. "Weren't you listening?"

"I heard all that," Arie gave an impatient shake of her head, "but I thought he'd been hired for that job. I didn't know he owned the whole shebang. The man 's a European billionaire." The words came out in a soft, almost reverent whisper. "I could see he was important, I just never guessed how much."

"Well, now you know." Lena walked over and perched on the side of Arie's desk. "And, like I said, way out of your league."

Arie grimaced, then heaved a dramatic sigh. "Maybe you're right. There's no way a man like him would be interested in someone like me."

"Maybe?" Lena cocked an eyebrow. "I'm always right." Then, shaking her head, she gave Arie a sympathetic smile. "That man moves in circles way different from ours. He probably doesn't even live here. We may never lay eyes on him again."

Arie's heart sank. That was a depressing thought, if there ever was one. It wasn't that she had her head in the clouds. Of course, she knew she didn't have the chance of a snowball in hell, but the thought that she would never see him again...

"Hey, this is some interesting stuff." Lena's words snapped Arie back to the present. As she spoke, Lena was peering at the monitor, then she reached out to tap the down arrow so the photo scrolled up, and more words appeared on the screen. "Italian, thirty-one years old, from the mega-rich Milano family in Italy. four generations rich. Crimey." She scrolled some more. "Hey, he went to school here. Got his MBA from Stanford. Nice."

Arie grimaced. Much good that would do her. The man was still inaccessible in so many more ways than one.

Why couldn't he have been from a humble background, a man who'd had to work to create his wealth? At least, that way he would have some sort of connection with ordinary folk like her. Better yet, why couldn't he have been an employee of the firm, a struggling artist or even a model? Anything except what he really was – way out of her reach.

Because, this weird attraction she had for him, it wasn't just his looks. There was something about him that she couldn't explain, something that just...clicked.

"And guess what?" Lena's chortle broke into her musings. "He's free, single and disengaged. How is that even possible?"

Arie groaned. "Don't rub it in, will you?" Reaching for the mouse, she clicked to close the screen, effectively removing from view the source of her distress. "I almost wish you'd said he was married. That would be sure to knock him out of my system real fast."

Lena laughed and leaned over to comfort Arie with a quick back rub. "It's okay, honey. You aren't the first to obsess over an inaccessible hottie and, trust me, you won't be the last. All part of growing up, my dear. You'll soon find a stable, stable, steady man who'll be home every evening by six." She got up off the desk, still sporting a smile. "And at the end of the day, you'll be glad you went for regular and reliable rather than suave and sexy. The sexy ones? Nothing but trouble, and I speak from experience." With a laugh and a shake of her head, she turned and headed back to her office.

That left Arie feeling even more depressed. Regular and reliable, Lena said. Somehow, that didn't appeal to her one bit. Perverse creature that she was, what really turned her on was hot, sexy and...

She shook her head, stopping herself before she went any further. It was just too bad, but she would be getting none of that, at least not today. She had a busy day ahead of her and the last thing she needed to be doing just then was wasting any more of her precious time, pining over Rome Milano.

Honestly, I need a life. Mumbling under her breath, Arie got up from behind her desk and headed for the door. She had a wedding to cater on the weekend and she needed to get some air. Now was the perfect time to run out and get all her errands done. That would be sure to pull her mind away from matters that were only getting her all hot and bothered.

She didn't get back to the office until almost five o'clock that afternoon and she was in good spirits. The fresh air had done her good, and on top of that, she'd found some great deals in Wedding Belles. It was her luck to go shopping for supplies the day they were having their after-Thanksgiving-and-getting-ready-for-Christmas sale.

"Hey, look at these," she called out, as she used her foot to nudge Lena's office door open. "White orchids. They're going to look great on the buffet table, don't you think?"

"Well, you're in a good mood."

As Arie turned, her arms full of bags, silk bouquets and streamers, Lena hopped up and ran to help her. "Come on, rest them over here."

With a happy sigh, Arie relinquished her load to her partner, her face beaming. "We've saved a lot of money this time and it will all be going to the bottom line."

"Sweet." Lena hurried over to plop the armload of supplies on top of her already crowded credenza. When she turned, there was a sly smile on her face. "But now, I have a spanking for you."

"For me? What did I do?" Arie gave her a mock frown. "Don't tell me I forgot to give you a receipt or something.

You're such a pain when it comes to book-keeping."

"No, you forgot your cell phone. As usual."

"Oh." Arie tapped the pocket of her slacks thought I had it on me."

"Nope, but you should have. I was trying to call you."

"Yeah? What about?" Arie shrugged out of her sweater and walked over to hook it on Lena's rack. "We got a last minute booking?"

"Better than that. Better for you, anyway." Lena gave her a mysterious look that made her frown.

"What's that supposed to mean? Hey, did you double book me?" She folded her arms and glared. "Tell me you didn't." "No, I didn't. I got a phone call for you."
"On my cell phone?"

"No, on the office line. I was trying to reach you on the cell to tell you about it." Lena's smile grew wider and even more mysterious. "Guess who called?"

"Oh, please. Not the guessing game. Just tell me, already. You know I hate it..."

"Rome Milano."

"...when you do that. You always..." The words caught in Arie's throat. Her eyes widened as she stared at Lena. "Did you just say Rome Milano?"

Lena gave her a super-satisfied grin. "I did."
"You're kidding, right?" Arie felt her heart jerk in her chest. "He doesn't even know me. Why would he call?" She sucked in her breath as a thought flashed into her mind. "Does this have anything to do with the event we catered for them? Was there a problem?"

"Didn't sound like there was a problem to me. His assistant was as chirpy as could be."

Arie narrowed her eyes. "I thought you said Rome Milano called."

Lena shrugged. "His office called. Same difference. Mr. Milano summoned you to a meeting tomorrow afternoon, three o'clock. I accepted on your behalf."

"A meeting?" Baffled, Arie cocked her head to one side as she stared at her friend. "What sort of meeting?"

Lena shook her head. "Don't ask me. But does it matter? You got what you've been dreaming of. You're going to see your man." Lena chuckled. "I thought you'd be jumping all over the place at the news. Aren't you excited?"

Slowly, Arie nodded, letting the news sink in. As she thought about it, her face melted into a smile, then broke into a wide grin. "Of course, I'm excited. I was just...in shock." Then, as another delicious thought slipped into her mind, she gazed off into space, losing herself in a momentary fantasy. "Maybe he likes me?"

That made Lena laugh out loud. "You're quite the dreamer, you know that?" She walked back to her desk and plopped down in her chair, still shaking her head as she smiled up at Arie. "One thing's for sure, you're not short on ambition."

Arie smiled back, but she didn't say a word. Out of the blue, she'd been blessed with this chance to see Rome Milano again. Right now, the gods were on her side, and she would not squander their gift.

If she played her cards right, she might just get a date with hottie Rome Milano, and it might just happen by the holidays.

. . ❧ . .

Rome picked up his cell phone and glanced at the time. Two fifty-six. In another four minutes, he would see his mystery woman again.

His personal assistant had set up the meeting and had even gone to the trouble of putting together a folder with a profile of the woman, including photo, résumé and more. Pity he hadn't had the chance to go through it. He'd come back from Italy two days later than planned, walking off the plane straight into a board meeting, and it had been non-stop meetings ever since. He'd only just got back from one three minutes earlier.

It didn't matter, though. He didn't need to see the girl's resume to know that she would be good at whatever task she was assigned. He could see it in the way she carried herself – back straight, mouth set in a determined line, eyes never wavering as she met your gaze, head-on. The girl was bold, and he could see she was business-like. She would be a great addition to any team. And the fact that she'd caught his interest in other ways was totally irrelevant.

At exactly three o'clock, he heard a knock at his door, and Iyana stuck her head in. "Miss Angelis is here to see you."

Excellent. His guest had passed the first test. She was right on time.

"Send her in." Rome got up from around his desk and walked across the four hundred square foot space. He always made it a point to meet his visitors at the door, and today would be no exception.

He was almost there, when Arie Angelis stepped in, looking nothing like when he'd first seen her. If anything, in her navy-blue tailored skirt suit, she looked even more stunning.

Her long, blonde hair was swept up in an elegant bun and her soft lips, now colored dusky pink, seemed fuller than he remembered. But those eyes, as blue and mysterious as the ocean, were still just as bold and just as direct. The girl didn't have a shy bone in her body.

"Miss Angelis." Rome held out his hand, and when she smiled and slid her soft one in his, he shook it and gave her a deferent nod. "Thank you for coming on such short notice."

"It's my pleasure," she said, her smile brightening ever so slightly, a hint color kissing her cheeks.

For one brief moment, he could not move, nor did he want to. He was no poet, but he would almost say her fresh-faced beauty was like the dawning of a brand new day. Captivating.

Realizing he'd been holding her hand just a little bit too long, Rome released her and directed her to a seat, then he circled the desk and sat down behind it. Sitting back in his chair, he propped his elbows on the arms and tented his fingers. "I imagine you're wondering why I asked you to come."

Her lips curled in a smile, and she gave a slight nod. "You could say that."

"I won't waste your time or mine. Let me get straight to the point." He sat forward in his chair and rested his folded arms on top of the desk. "How much money do you make per hour?"

Arie's eyebrows shot up, then her brows knotted in a frown. "Excuse me?"

"I asked you how much money you make. What? Five bucks an hour? Six?"

Her smile long gone, Arie stared back at Rome in obvious confusion. "Um...why? What does that have to do with our meeting?"

Rome gave her a confident smile. "It's got everything to do with our meeting. I've got a proposal for you." He sat back in his chair again, his eyes never leaving her face. "As a server, you probably make five or six dollars an hour plus tips, with little chance of moving up the ladder. How would you like to work for me instead?"

"Excuse me?" she asked again, looking even more confused.

He laughed. "What? Too good to be true? I thought you'd jump at the chance to make some real money." When she didn't answer right away, he continued. "I know you're wondering what I've got in mind. Don't worry. This position is perfect for you. My company needs an event planner, and I have no doubt that you have all the skills necessary."

That seemed to draw a reaction, but instead of the smile of joy he was expecting, her lips tightened and her brows fell. Instead of effusive expressions of gratitude, Arie Angelis fixed him with a glare so cold, he knew he'd pissed her off.

"Is that what you called me here for? To offer me a job?"

That made him pause. What did she think he'd called her in for? A tête-à-tête? "Look, Miss Angelis, this is strictly business. I'm making you a very attractive job offer. You would make several times the pay you're getting now." As he stared back at her, Rome could not stop himself from frowning. Miss Angelis had accepted his meeting invitation right away, and he knew part of that quick response was because of that fleeting but real connection they'd shared the first time they met. In offering her a job, he was not only creating an opportunity for them to actually get to know each other, but he was also opening up a wide world of opportunity for her. She would actually be able to make a good living. Didn't she see that?

"And what makes you think I'm a server?" She lifted an eyebrow but there was no mirth in her eyes.

"You were serving, weren't you?" His frown deteriorated into a scowl. What was her problem? He'd been so confident she would jump at his offer, he hadn't even contemplated the possibility of her refusal. But now, with her display of attitude, she was really getting on his nerves.

"Miss Angelis," he said, his voice cool ,and the look he gave her even cooler, "I'll only say this one more time. I'm offering you a full-time position here at Belitalia. The salary and benefits far exceed the market average. Take it or leave it."

Rome watched the emotions flit across Arie's face, and for the life of him, he could not figure out what she was thinking. At first, he saw what looked like a flash of anger ,and then he saw doubt, but then her brows smoothed, and a hint of a smile touched her lips.

He almost smiled back. The girl was finally coming around, and it made sense. She would be a fool if she didn't.

"Mr. Milano, thank you so much for your job offer,"
she said, her face suddenly soft and even pleasant,
"but I'll leave it."

"Smart move," he said, as his face broke into a smile. And then he stopped. "You'll what?"

"I'll leave it," she said, her face still pleasant, her smile growing wider. "Thank you."

And with that, she got up, turned around and walked right out of his office.

"What the..." For several seconds, Rome just sat there, staring at the closed door. "Well, I'll be damned."

As the words left his lips, he got up and shoved his chair back, then stalked across the room. He was about to march through the open door , when he checked himself. Just in time. How the hell would it look if he went after her? No. Wasn't going to happen. It would be a cold day in hell, before he went running after a woman, particularly a dimwitted one who didn't know a good thing when it was handed to her on a silver platter.

Shoving his hands in his pockets, Rome gave a grunt of annoyance and walked back to his desk. He wasn't used to rejection, not from anyone, and definitely not from a woman.

He shook his head, for once in his life utterly confused. He was used to members of the opposite sex falling all over themselves to get to him. So, what was it with this one?

Rome drew in his breath then let it out slowly, and as his surprise and anger subsided , he laughed and shook his head.

He'd probably just met one of the few women in the world who could tell him no.

And that made him all the more intrigued.

Some way, somehow, he would have to get to the bottom of this one. Whether she liked it or not, he would have to see her again.

CHAPTER THREE

T he nerve of the man, to think that all he had to do was drop a job offer in her lap and she would fall, swooning at his feet in gratitude. What did he take her for?

It was an infuriated Arie who marched into the office next day. She was taking Rome's behavior as an insult, and it had already colored her day. And the color was the fiery-red of rage.

"Hey, what's up with you?" Lena swiveled around from the reception counter and stared at her as she walked in, slamming the door behind her. "Got up on the wrong side of the bed?"

"I hate men." Arie shrugged out of her sweater, and instead of hanging it on the rack at the entrance, she threw it onto the coffee table in the reception area. Today, she was in no mood to be neat. "That's what I get for liking a man who's too pretty."

That made Lena cock a curious eyebrow. "With that speech. it's a good thing the receptionist isn't in yet. I could just see her gobbling up this juicy bit of gossip." She jerked her head toward her office. "Come on in and let's talk."

Inside, Lena poured Arie a cup of tea, then sat down to hear the full story. "So, tell me what's pissed you off this time. I'm guessing your meeting with Rome Milano didn't go too well."

Arie gave a snort. "You got that right. It didn't go well at all. I thought the man was calling me to a meeting to discuss business. You know, one business leader to another." Too annoyed to want to sit there, ,sipping tea, she deposited the cup and saucer on Lena's desk. "I'm a leader in my field, just like he is. Why couldn't he take me seriously?"

Lena frowned. "So, what did he do? Make a pass at you?" Lena's face darkened. "Just say the word, and I'll have my lawyer on him so fast, he won't know what hit him. Big shot or no, he can't do that and get away with it."

"No, he didn't make a pass at me." Arie grimaced. "I almost wish that was it."

"Then what?" Lena's dark eyes were filled with confusion. "What did he do that made you so upset?"

Arie grimaced again, then she gave a grunt of disgust. "He offered me a job."

For several seconds, Lena stared at her, the confusion never leaving her face, then she shook her head. "Okay, so let me understand this. Rome Milano pissed the hell out of you because...he offered you a job?"

"It's not just that, Lena. The man offered me a job as an event planner with his firm. And do you know why? He thought it would be a huge step up for me. A step up from my current job as a server."

Lena stared at her some more, then she smiled. "So, you're pissed that he thought you were a server. He didn't acknowledge you as one of the owners of Talkof the Town."

"Now, do you understand why I'm so upset?" Arie shook her head. "I know exactly why he made that assumption. It's because I'm blonde."

"Oh, come on, Arie. Give the man the benefit of the doubt."

"No, I won't. I'm sick and tired of people...especially men...making assumptions about me, simply because of the way I look." The more Arie thought about it, the more she bristled. "And that's exactly what he did. I couldn't be anything but a server. Too blonde, he probably said, or too pretty."

Lena gave a soft chuckle. "Have a sip of your tea, Arie, before you burst. Come on. Right now." She raised an eyebrow and Arie knew she wouldn't be allowed to say another word until she'd followed instructions. So, still grumbling, she picked up the cup and sipped.

Lena gave a nod of approval. "Now that you're a little calmer, let me remind you of something." She gave Arie a patient smile. "On the night of the event, you were serving, weren't you?"

"Sure, but I was just helping out."

"And how was he supposed to know that?" Lena's smile widened. "That night you were head cook and bottle washer, remember? In the middle of everything. And, besides," Lena's smile turned sly, "you were grabbing trays and slipping into the banquet hall every chance you got, so you could spy on the man. No wonder he thought you were one of the servers."

Arie glared back at Lena. Her partner had a point, but she wasn't ready to concede and she definitely wasn't ready to forgive Rome Milano. "Well, he went to the trouble of tracking me down and inviting me to a meeting. He should have done his research and found out who I really was. You would think that would be step one."

Lena tilted her head. "You do have a point. That, I can't explain. But trust me, the man wasn't trying to insult you, and your being blonde had absolutely nothing to do with his blunder, okay? You've always been so sensitive about that. You're blonde and you're beautiful. Deal with it."

And with that, she got up and proceeded to shoo Arie out of her office. "Now, take your tea with you and get out of my office. I have a meeting with the auditors this morning and I have to get ready." As Arie went through the door, she called out, "And take your mind off that man. He's not worth your being upset all day."

"Easy for you to say," Arie grumbled under her breath. But, like Lena ordered, she went off to her office to tackle her million and one tasks for the day.

And the day flew by so fast that it was soon three o'clock and she was only on the third item on her list of things to do, a list that boasted all of twelve tasks. Arie could only sigh and dig in again, trying to go that much faster.

She was in the middle of reviewing a catering contract for a series of banquets at the Hyacinth Hotel, when the phone on her desk began to ring. Not even looking up from her paperwork, she grabbed the receiver and jammed it to her ear. "Arie Angelis speaking."

"Miss Angelis, I have a gentleman here to see you." Marilyn's voice sounded soft and breathless, not at all like the receptionist she'd known almost two years.

Arie frowned. She was just about to ask Marilyn if she was okay, but she didn't. That would just sound too odd. "Who is it, Marilyn?" she asked, hoping it wasn't Larry Brown from the advertising firm next door. The man had a habit of dropping in for a chat, which was annoying, to say the least, but especially today.

"It's Mr. Milano...from Belitalia." The woman's voice was breathless with awe.

Arie's grip on the receiver tightened and she sat up straight in her chair. "Rome Milano...is here to see me?" "Yes. I...should I send him in?"

"Uh...yes. please."

Arie hung up the phone then, quick as a flash, she began to straighten up the mess on her desk. She didn't have a reputation for neatness, and things usually got real bad when she was under pressure, with papers strewn everywhere.

The thing was, it was usually Lena who had the visitors, not her. She hardly ever had to worry about tidying up to receive guests. Unfortunately, today - when she was at her busiest and most untidy - was the exception.

She'd grabbed a particularly messy folder, when there was a knock at the door. Arie dropped the file on the floor and used her toe to shove it under her desk. "Come in," she called out, her voice a study in calm, cool confidence.

The door opened, and in the next instant, the tall, Armani-suited frame of Rome Milano filled the entrance. And, just like she'd expected, at the sight of him, her heart did a little skip inside her chest. There was nothing she could do to stop this attraction she felt for this oh, so super-sexy man. What she would give, to have him in her bed...

Still, she was a pretty good actress so, feigning composure, she walked toward her surprise visitor. "Mr. Milano. Welcome to Talk of the Town. To what do I owe the pleasure?"

"Call me Rome," he said, with a slight bow of the head, and then he took her hand.

If he'd wanted to throw her off balance, he was doing a darned good job. Just his touch was enough to send her pulse racing and make her nipples go pebble-hard. And, not to mention those piercing brown eyes that never ceased to send thrills up and down her spine.

When he released her, it was all she could do to keep from shoving her hand inside her pocket to hide it from view. The last thing she needed was for the man to see the effect he was having on her.

"Mr. Milano," she said with a nod, "come in, please. Have a seat." Waving him over to the empty chair, she escaped to the safety of her desk. She was more than happy to hide behind that shield.

Once he'd settled in his seat she drew in a stealthy, calming breath and put on her 'woman-in-charge' face. "So," she said, with a lift of her eyebrows, "how may I help you?"

Rome relaxed his lithe, lean body in the chair, then gave her a slow, almost sultry smile that oozed confidence and charm. It was bad enough that the man was so sinfully handsome. Did he have to be so darned smooth as well? "Miss Angelis," he said, then paused and cocked an eyebrow. "May I call you Arie?" At her nod, he continued. "Arie, I'm here because I want to apologize."

That made Arie's ears perk up. "Apologize?"

"Yes. I owe you an apology for not doing my homework." His smile disappeared and his face turned serious. "Aristotle Angelis, co-founder and owner of Talk of the Town, the number one catering company in the State of Louisiana. I should have known this when you walked into my office yesterday. I'm sorry."

"Oh." She was so surprised at his apology that, for the moment, she was lost for words. In her head, she'd created such an ugly picture of him – jerk, ogre, male chauvinist pig – that his apology threw her totally off balance.

As if he didn't even notice her confusion, Rome continued speaking. "I've been accused more than once of being a chauvinist." He gave her a crooked smile. "Yesterday was a demonstration of that." His smile softened sexily, and he gave her a look that was hard to resist. "Let me make it up to you," He said softly, almost seductively. "Have dinner with me. Please."

Another surprise. For a second, Arie stared at him in disbelief, and then she shook her head. "I don't think so."

Now, it was his turn to seem surprised. The sudden lift of an eyebrow, the slight twist of his lips, they were enough to tell her that Rome Milano was not used to being turned down. But he recovered soon enough, his smile returning full force. "Are you going to make me beg?"

Enjoying having the upper hand, Arie shrugged casually. "Sounds good."

Rome laughed, and it was a comfortable, genuine laugh that had her smiling back. "Okay then, I'll beg. Aristotle Angelis, will you have dinner with me? I'm begging."

That made her laugh and, whether it was the wisest decision or not, there was no way she could turn him down now.

Still, she had to rub it in just a little more. "Hmm, I don't know..." She rubbed her chin as if deep in thought.

"Please." Rome shook his head, still smiling. "Do I need to get down on one knee?"

Now, that would be too much. She could just imagine the wild fantasies that would start flying around in her head if he ever did something like that. And, as she well knew, those over-the-top fantasies would never come true. Not in this life, anyway. "No, don't," she said quickly, when it looked like he was about to do what he'd just threatened. "I accept."

"Thank you." Rome gave her a satisfied look that had her thinking, the man was a master manipulator; that much was clear. But she could manipulate, too. Little did he know it.

Because, when you looked at it, it was she who'd gotten what she wanted. For some reason, the stars were lined up in her favor and, just like she'd dreamed, she would be seeing more of Rome, the looker.

Within minutes, they'd agreed on date, time and location for their date and Arie couldn't have been more pleased. She was just wrapping up those plans with Rome, when there was a tap at the door, and Lena peeked in. "Sorry to disturb," she said with an apologetic smile, "but I need a file from your cabinet. I'll only be a sec."

31

"Lena, come on in." Arie waved her friend into the office. "Meet Rome Milano, CEO of Belitalia. We catered their sales award banquet, remember?"

"I remember." Lena walked over and held out her hand, her smile widening when Rome stood up and towered over her. Lena was tall and there were few men who could do that. Arie could see that she was tickled by it. "I saw you at the banquet, but it's good to meet you face to face, Mr. Milano."

"Call me Rome," he said, as he took her hand. "I'm impressed with the service Talk of the Town provides. You'll be hearing from my planning manager for future events."

"I look forward to it." Lena gave him a parting smile and

turned to head for the cabinet. Rome turned back to Arie. "So, Saturday night. Eight o'clock."

Arie nodded. "I'll see you then."

That settled, he gave her a nod, then turned toward the door.

Arie made to follow, but he stopped her. "That's okay. I'll see myself out." He looked over to where Lena stood, her look a mixture of surprise and curiosity. "Have a good afternoon," he said, nodding to both of them, and then he turned and was out the door.

Immediately, Lena's face broke into a huge grin. "A date?" she whispered, looking almost as excited as Arie was feeling. She nodded, knowing that Lena was probably busy trying to figure out how she'd pulled that off.

Feeling pleased as rum punch, Arie gave Lena a cheeky smile. "And that," she said, with a self-satisfied grin, "is how you do it."

Saturday night could not come fast enough for Arie but then, when it finally came, she began to feel just a little bit uneasy. She'd gotten what she wanted, but now, she didn't feel quite so bold. She was good at exuding confidence when she wanted to impress, but the real Arie was actually quite shy.

The doubts came flying in from left and right. What if he didn't like her? What if she got nervous and made a fool of herself? God forbid, but what if he was one of those who held on to stereotypes about blondes? Would that color his opinion of her?

Arie shook her head. "Enough," she muttered, then grabbed her purse and marched out of the house before she turned chicken and called him to cancel the date.

They'd agreed to meet at M. Bistro at the Ritz Carlton Hotel and when Arie walked into the lobby, Rome was already there, looking as suave and composed as she'd expected.

As soon as he saw her, he gave her an easy smile and walked over. "You look lovely tonight," he said, his eyes roaming over her, making every inch of her tingle.

She'd been stared at before, but never quite like this. The way Rome was looking at her, made her feel like she was the most beautiful creature on earth...one he was eager to woo.

As if tuned in to her thoughts, like a courtly gentleman, Rome took her hand and rested it in the crook of his arm. "Shall we dine, madam?" He gave her a look of amusement.

She gave him a quick nod and a quick smile. "Why, I think we shall," she said, playing along with his game. But then, she spoiled it by laughing. "I don't know if that came out right. Was that a good British accent?"

"Pretty decent." He was probably being kind, but their little farce was all it took to put her at ease. At least, the man had some semblance of humor.

That night, Arie and Rome dined on sweet corn ravioli, gumbo, salmon and roasted chicken. The food was exquisite, but that wasn't the best part of the date. What Arie loved was the way Rome opened up to her, telling her little things about himself that made her look at him in a totally different light. She'd thought he was egotistical and jaded, the product of a privileged upbringing, but there was a boyish side to him, a humorous side that had her cracking up.

As she dipped her spoon into the crème brûlée, Arie looked over at Rome and, unable to stifle her curiosity any longer, she said, "You don't seem to have much of an Italian accent. How come?"

He smiled. "I've spent so many years in the United States, sometimes I feel more American than Italian."

She dabbed at her lips with her napkin. "What do you mean?"

I went to high school in Atlanta, where our old office was located, and then I did my first degree as well as grad school here." He shrugged. "I love the old country, but I also call America home. I've got the best of both worlds, I guess."

She nodded. "So, do you spend more time in Europe or here? Sounds like you've got offices across the globe."

"And excellent managers to run them. I divide most of my time between Europe and the United States, and I visit my Latin American and Asian operations about once each quarter. Lately, I've been spending quite a bit of time right here." He gave her an enigmatic smile. "Maybe that's a good thing."

He was looking at her so intently, that Arie dropped her gaze and picked up her spoon again, feigning renewed interest in her dessert.

"And what about you?"

At his question, she looked up again. "I'm sorry?"

"Where'd you get a name like Aristotle? It would be unusual enough applied to a modern-day man, but to a woman?" He cocked an eyebrow. "Forgive me, but it does beg the question."

She smiled, glad for the change in subject. "Blame it on my mother. I don't know her, but I was told she was very much into all things Greek and, on top of that, she thought that I looked wise. So, now I'm stuck with this weird moniker." She shook her head. "Just my luck.

She'd thought Rome would laugh, or maybe joke around about her name – a blonde woman with a name like Aristotle?

She'd heard it all before, so she was used to the teasing, and she was ready.

But it never came. Instead, he was frowning. "You don't know your mother?"

That caught her off guard. She hadn't expected him to latch on to that part of the story. That wasn't usually what caught the attention. "No, I was given up for adoption at birth." Then, not wanting him to feel sorry for her, she added, "But I had a pretty good childhood, and now that I'm grown up and independent, things could not be better."

Of course, if she were to be perfectly honest, they could. It sucked that she had no idea who her mother was, nor who any of her relatives were, for that matter. It sucked that when she had problems, she was on her own. And it sucked that when the holidays came around, she had nowhere to go, except maybe to Lena's.

But all that was for her to know and keep under her hat. She gave him a brilliant smile designed to show him that she meant it, that things were great.

It usually worked, but not this time. "Tell me about that," Rome said. "Your life, your childhood." And then, he sat back in his chair, looking like he was prepared to hear her whole life story. The man was actually curious. Who would have thought it?

She shrugged. "There's not much to tell. I grew up in five foster homes, and when I was eighteen, I went out on my own. I've been living an independent life ever since."

"And you're good with that?"

"I'm...good with that." She was repeating what he'd said but she was staring back at him, half-confused. What kind of question was that? She had to be good with it. What choice did she have?

"You've never been tempted to start a family of your own?" His dark eyes were intense. She could not plumb their depths.

Suddenly feeling flustered, she looked away. Then, she shook her head. "I guess...I never found the right man." Feeling totally uncomfortable with the direction the conversation had taken, Arie desperately fished around for something else to talk about, anything that would get Rome's mind off her. "I hear there's a great jazz band here. Want to check it out?" She gazed at him wistfully, hoping he would take her bait.

"Sure. Why not? The night's still young."

As Rome waved for the check, Arie stifled a sigh of relief. That was close. She hoped he would never go down that road again. Definitely too personal.

Within minutes, they were heading for the lounge where, to Arie's delight, they found jazz trumpeter and vocalist, Jeremy Davenport, in live performance.

"There's a free table right up front," Rome whispered. "Let's grab those seats then I'll order some drinks."

It was such a treat, Arie could not have been more grateful to Rome for taking her to the Ritz Carlton that night. Just sitting there, listening to Jeremy Davenport croon the words of Satchmo's classic, 'It's a Wonderful World', had her in such a mellow mood, she could have stayed there all night. Then, when he pulled out his trumpet and began to she was one of the first to lift her hands in applause.

"You like jazz."

It wasn't a question, but a statement, and Arie did not hesitate to nod. "Love it. I could listen to this every day." Feet tapping, her fingers rapping the table, she was so in tune with the music, she could not stay still. When the trumpeter switched to the music of Nigerian legend, Sade, her face broke into an even wider smile. How did the musician know Sade was one of her jazz favorites?

When Rome laid his hand on top of hers, Arie jumped.

"Come on," he said. "Let's dance."

"But I don't dance." Arie gave him a doubtful look.

"Don't give me that. You're practically hopping out of your seat." Rome got up, pulling her with him. "I won't take no for an answer."

Seeing that he was determined to take her onto the dance floor, Arie swallowed her embarrassment and walked dutifully behind him. She couldn't remember the last time she'd actually gone dancing. She could only pray she didn't trip and fall flat on her face.

But then, Rome put his arms around her, and as the muted trumpet caressed the rhythm of 'Your Love Is King', he began to sway to the sensual sounds, pulling her close, making her follow his every move.

The music was like waves of sweet sensation washing over her, and Arie soon felt the tension in her dissolve until she was relaxing into Rome, her body reveling in that first touch, the feel of his long, lean body, so solid against hers.

ROME FOR THE HOLIDAYS

The dance floor was filling up and Arie was glad, because she and Rome were soon lost in a crowd of couples holding each other and swaying to the silky sounds. They were anonymous, unknown, just one of the many who had not been able to resist the pull of the melodies.

But, before Arie knew what was happening, it was not the music that was carrying her away, but the feel of Rome's arms around her, the fragrance of his fresh-scented cologne, the beat of his heart as she laid her cheek against his chest.

Then, as if under the same spell, Rome's arms tightened around her and he dipped his head to brush his lips against her heated brow, making her mouth go dry.

Rome's lips slid down to tickle her ear. "Let's get out of here." It was a raspy whisper, one that breathed the desire he must have been feeling at that moment.

If he was feeling anything like she was, he was having a hard time keeping his hands to himself. Because that was exactly how she was feeling about him.

Rome gave her his hand and, without hesitation, she took it then turned to follow him off the dance floor. She had no idea where they were going and she didn't care, as long as it was some place where they could be alone.

It didn't take her long to find out. Rome must have been very familiar with the layout of the Ritz Carlton because, within a minute of leaving the lounge, they were in a secluded alcove bathed in shadows. There, Rome put his hand on her shoulders and turned her to face him.

"I want to kiss you," he said, his face hidden in the shadows, leaving her to guess at his state of arousal. It wasn't hard, though. If the breathlessness of his whisper and his grip on her shoulders were anything to go by, he was just as turned on as she was. "May I, mada?"

He was playing courtly gentleman again and Arie was game. "Yes, sir," she whispered back. "You most certainly may." Rome gave a soft sigh of satisfaction and then his hands slid over to cup her face as he gazed down at her. Then, slowly,

so excruciatingly slowly, he lowered his mouth to hers.

At the touch of his lips, Arie's nipples puckered into pointy peaks, turning hard as pebbles in her bra. She moaned against his mouth and, as if in answer to her unspoken plea, he slid his hands down to span her waist and draw her even closer to him.

Their bodies touched, and the feel of him pressed against her, sent her emotions into a tailspin. Trembling at his touch, she slid her hands up so she could cling to him and draw from his strength as he stroked her senses with his kiss.

With her in his arms, Rome took full control of the kiss, molding his lips to hers then, as she sighed and opened to him, teasing her with soft licks, then sliding in to taste her and tempt her, stealing her breath away.

When he finally drew his lips away and lifted his head to gaze down at her, Arie could only stare up at him with semiglazed eyes, unable to say a word.

His arms still wrapped around her, Rome gave her a smooth, seductive smile. "And that," he said, his voice a husky whisper, "is how you do it."

It took a second for the words to register, but when they did, Arie blinked. *Oh, my God. He heard me.* As the thought flashed through her mind, she stared up at him, wide-eyed.

But she could read nothing in his hooded gaze.

And as she dipped her head and drew back and out of his arms, she bit her lip, wishing she could take back those casually spoken words which now sounded so smug.

CHAPTER FOUR

I

It wasn't like she was the first beautiful woman who had caught his eye. It was not her beauty that was holding him captive. It was something mysterious, something a whole lot more curious that was doing him in.

And, typical Rome Milano, he would not stop until he'd figured things out. He had to see her again. "I don't see how this strategy will do us any good. It's more trouble than it's worth."

Rome's gaze snapped back to the charts projected on the screen, trying to tune in to what his senior VP of Finance was saying as he stood at the front of the conference room.

"If you look at the figures, you'll see that they tell the whole story. We started out in a strong position, but look at this dip." Eaton Knight directed the laser pointer to the lowest point on the graph. "Why did this happen?"

When Knight gave Rome a pointed look, he knew his senior VP was looking for back-up.

Rome looked around the room, taking in the doubtful expression on the Marketing V's face, t he operations manager shaking his head and the general manager's look, one of stubborn belligerence. If he didn't step in, he knew they would be here another two hours, debating the next move.

He understood the dynamics of the meeting. Every one of his managers wanted to look good, like he was the one who'd solved the problem and saved the company from a disastrous decision. But the problem was, each of them was viewing the problem from his own perspective. Not even the general manager was looking at the overall picture. And no amount of discussion would make them agree.

"Okay, team, this is what we'll do." There was no way Rome was going to sit through another two hours debating one issue. "This project is dead in the water. We'll abandon it and start fresh. Eaton, as the finance man, I want you to spearhead a new drive to introduce the men's formal line in Southeast Asia. Let's get the costing right, before we make any other move."

That said, he got up from the conference table and headed for the door.

"You're leaving?" The GM looked like he wanted to stop him before he left the room.

"That's right," Rome said, not slowing his stride. "There are other things that need my attention."

Not least of which was the need to get away and clear his head. His mind had been wandering too much, lately, and if there was ever a time he needed to burn some rubber on the highway and let the wind clear the cobwebs, this was it.

He'd just stepped back into his office, intent on grabbing his keys and heading out the door, when Iyana came in. "Rome, I have a message for you."

"Who from?" He wasn't eager to hear the answer. Whenever things were going smoothly, he hardly ever heard from his team. The problems, though, they gladly dropped on his table.

"It's from Aristotle Angelis." Iyana raised an eyebrow as she read the name from the note in her hand. "She wants you to meet her at her office in the French Quarter at three o'clock this afternoon."

On hearing the name, Rome stopped in his tracks. And then he frowned. That sounded like an order. He looked back at Iyana. "It's almost two o'clock."

"I know." She nodded and gave him a look of chagrin. "I should have said you were unavailable." She turned to go. "I'll call them back right now."

"No."

Iyana turned and gave him a quizzical look. "No? You're going to attend on this short notice?" "Yes. Don't worry about it. I'll make it by three."

Iyana frowned then folded her arms and shook her head. "And what about lunch? When were you planning on having that?"

He shrugged. "I'll grab something on the way. I'll be all right."

Iyana glared at him a moment longer then, with a grunt that sounded like annoyance, she turned and headed back to her own office.

"And when you get sick, please don't come running to me for the pink stuff." She was grumbling as she went out the door.

Rome grinned. Right now, Iyana was in 'mothering' mode, but there was nothing he could do about that. He had the chance to see Arie in little more than an hour and he was not about to turn that down.

And now, he was darned curious about her. When they'd parted, she'd seemed suddenly shy, even withdrawn. Now, though, it was like she'd made a one hundred and eighty degree turn. Unapologetically and with no notice at all, she'd just summoned him to her office.

What the heck was she up to?

"COME IN." ARIE HELD her breath as she waited for Rome to come into her office. All week, she'd been on edge, dying to see him again. Well, she wasn't going to wait any longer.

On impulse, she'd had her receptionist call his office and invite him to meet with her and, while awaiting his response, she'd had her fingers crossed behind her back. When Marilyn came in and told her the meeting was on, she'd almost given in to the urge to smile. Instead, she'd pretended to be oh, so composed and had simply given her receptionist a nod of acknowl- edgement, but inside she'd been hopping up and down with glee, knowing that today she would see him again.

Now that he was at her door she could practically feel her pupils dilating. Struggling to calm her nerves she drew in a steadying breath and got up from around her desk. Just like he'd done for her, she would walk over to meet him.

She was halfway to the door when it opened and there, in front of her, stood the man who had occupied her every waking thought.

She should be used to seeing Rome by now, used to the fact that he was as close to perfect as she'd ever seen any man. But as she gazed at him it was like she was seeing him for the first time – the shock of dark hair falling across his wide forehead, the lips so firm but so mobile, and those eyes. Always the eyes. Deep, dark pools that you could drown in... and gladly. Damn, the man looked good.

But then, realizing she was staring, Arie swallowed then gave Rome a welcoming smile. "Glad you could make it," she said as she stepped aside and waved him in.

She could see he had no idea why she'd called him in. There was a look of uncertainty in his eyes that told her she'd thrown him off balance. She liked that. Sometimes it was good to keep a man guessing...

> ...especially since she'd always been the 'good girl' but today she'd decided to be bad.

Now with the office door closed they were alone, just standing there in the middle of the room staring at each other, neither of them saying a word.

> Then, before she could change her mind, Arie made her move.

Walking right up to Rome she grabbed him by the lapels and pulled him close. "Kiss me," she said, "and that's an or- der."

Recovering quickly, Rome gave her his signature smile. "With pleasure, madam."

When he dipped his head toward her Arie did not wait passively for his kiss. She'd been waiting all week for this and now it was time for her to go for what she wanted.

Taking control, she reached up to cup his face in her hands then, applying pressure, she drew him down till his breath tickled her lips. She didn't wait for him to kiss her. Instead she kissed him, tilting her face up to capture his mouth with her own.

Releasing his face, she withdrew her hands to slide her fingers through the smoothness of his hair then, cupping the back of his head, she held him captive, holding him still while she took her fill of his lips.

Arie did not wait for Rome to recover. She released his lips just long enough to turn him around and back him closer and closer to the desk.

When his lips curled in a wicked smile Arie knew he'd guessed what she was up to. She wanted more.

Releasing him for just a second she grabbed an armful of folders from her desk, clearing some room, then she was back on him, giving him a quick shove that was enough to make him plop his rear onto the smooth, bare surface.

Rome reached for her then, pulling her to stand between his legs, looking like he was ready to take the lead. But she wouldn't let him.

As soon as she'd positioned herself in front of him Arie planted her hands on his shoulders, keeping him still, then she bent her head to trail nibbles and kisses up the side of his neck.

"Oh God, Arie. That feels good."

She knew it did. She could feel his body shiver at her teasing caress. So, pressing her advantage, she leaned over and treated the other side to the same sweet service, making his breath catch in his throat and his heart pound beneath her hands.

With a growl of frustration Rome slid off the desk and in one smooth move he'd turned then lifted her onto the surface he'd just vacated. "Enough with this teasing," he said in a heated whisper. "I want more."

Rome dipped his head and his lips had just touched the smoothness below her collarbone when there was a knock at the door.

They both froze.

A millisecond later, Rome was up and away from her, pulling his jacket down and straightening his tie. Arie swiftly slid off the desk and did some quick straightening of her own.

"Ready?" she whispered as she struggled to regain her composure.

At his nod she pasted a smile on her face and walked back around to her chair. "Come on in," she called out, her face totally composed.

But when she looked over at Rome her heart did a flip-flop. His lips were the fiery bronze she'd chosen to wear that

day.

Arie grabbed the box of tissues and threw it at him even as she hopped out of the chair to hurry forward and distract

her visitor.

Thankfully, he was on the ball, making a quick swipe at his lips as she took the folder from Marilyn's hand. The woman threw a curious glance at the back of Rome's head but Arie shooed her out so fast she didn't get more than a fleeting look.

When she closed the door she sagged against it, fighting to swallow the laughter that threatened to spill over. When she finally tore herself away from the door she was still shaking with suppressed laughter and she saw that Rome was, too.

"That's what happens," she whispered, "when you have a nosy receptionist." Smiling, Rome shook his head. "Next time," he said, "we'll do this at my place."

That made Arie tingle all over. Rome was looking as eager as she was feeling, and as far as 'next time' was concerned, she could hardly wait.

CHAPTER FIVE

Rome was still having a hard time believing what had happened in Arie's office. The girl knew how to take charge, and he loved it.

And by the time he'd left her office, they had date number two all arranged. This time, though, it would be a quiet affair. Cooking was Arie's passion, apparently, and she'd been eager to invite him to her house, where she would make him a pre-Christmas dinner, an Italian one at that. She'd promised it would take him right back home.

December twenty-first couldn't come around fast enough for Rome. He was amused at how eager he was to see Arie again. Feeling like an infatuated schoolboy, he jumped into his Maserati and headed out to her house. This, he knew, would be a Saturday to remember. Good food and a lovely lady to share it with. What better way to spend the evening?

It didn't take long before he was pulling into the driveway of Arie's home, just outside the city limits. Luckily, it was one of the few areas that hadn't been devastated by the flooding that had come with the a recent hurricane. It was a beautiful property with manicured lawns that spread out on both sides of the tree-lined drive, and neat flowerbeds nestling around the house. The home itself seemed like it had been around for over a century, but it was obviously well-kept and would be worth a fair bit of money on the market.

Rome was impressed. He'd expected to be invited to a modest home in Lakeview or the French Quarter, but this was a big surprise. Although young, he could see that Arie had done well for herself, and without the help of family. Despite the fact that he'd known her for little over a month, he'd seen what she was capable of, and he was darned proud of her achievements. With a smile of approval, he reached for the bottle of Dom Pérignon, got out of the car, and headed toward the house.

The woman who greeted him at the door was the picture of elegance. Sheathed in an ankle-length shift of black and gold, her hair coiled on top of her head, with soft tendrils framing her face, to Rome she'd never looked prettier. And then she smiled, looking even lovelier, her soft pink lips curving into a pretty bow, her blue eyes sparkling as she gazed up at him. God, he wanted to kiss her so bad.

"Come in," she said, and took the bottle from his hand. "You didn't have to do this, but thank you." Then she came close, smelling like sunset and roses, and went on tiptoe to give him a soft kiss on the cheek. "Welcome to Bayou House."

"Thank you," he said, with a smile and a nod. "And is there a bayou here?"

"There is," she said, as she led the way down the spacious marble-tiled hallway. "Way out back. But I'm also blessed with a tiny stream on the property. We can take a walk down there before dinner."

That idea appealed to Rome. When it came to romantic walks, what could beat a stroll by a bubbling brook in New Orleans?

But, to his disappointment, the evening was just cool enough for Arie to drape a scarf over her shoulders, but not so cool that she needed his arms around her. He would have welcomed the excuse to hold her close. He would have to be patient, he guessed. If all went as he hoped, he would have her in his arms soon enough.

The stream was not a disappointment, though.. Gently flowing and crystal-clear, it was what a poet would describe as a delight. With the air so cool and the butterflies flitting from flower to flower, this idyllic scene was enough to add another ten percent to the value of the property. The walk was refreshing, and ended up being quite the appetite booster. As they left the quiet stream and made their way back to the house, Rome's stomach betrayed him with an embarrassing growl.

Arie laughed out loud, her bright eyes flashing in the dying rays of the setting sun. "I won't keep you waiting a minute longer," she said. "Come on. Race you back to the porch."

Before he could even react, she was off, tearing across the lawn, looking like a fairy floating on the wind. With a laugh, Rome set off after her, but it was no use. The girl was small, but deceptively quick. Within seconds, she was hopping up and down on the porch, gloating at her victory.

"You lose," she cried, clapping her hands in glee. "That means you do the dishes."

"Hey, no fair." He came to a panting halt at the foot of the steps. "You didn't tell me there was a penalty."

"It doesn't matter. You still couldn't have beat me." With a grin and a haughty look of superiority, she turned and sauntered sexily back into the house, leaving him to humbly follow in her wake.

The meal Arie had prepared was well worth the wait. Tonight, she was treating him to a true Italian feast. To his surprise, she'd gone through all the trouble of preparing traditional Italian Christmas Eve fare, which included all of seven different types of fish. Thank God, she hadn't gone over that number. There were still regions in Italy where Christmas Eve dinner included up to eleven or even thirteen varieties. Tonight, he was hungry, but thirteen different varieties of fish? Not that hungry.

"I made you La Vigilia Napoletane," she said, as she ladled the portions onto his plate. "I wanted to remind you of home." She was smiling as she filled his plate, but it was a smile so wistful that it touched Rome's heart. "I guess you and your family have this every year at Christmas time," she continued, "like a family tradition, right?"

Rome was looking up at her, but she'd gazed away, seeming momentarily lost in a world of her own. "Yes, we do," he said, .as he watched the emotions flit across her face. "I've had Christmas broccoli and fried eel all of the thirty-one Christmases I've been on this earth."

"Nice," she said softly, almost absent-mindedly, as if she hadn't heard him and her thoughts were far away. Then, she blinked, and when she looked down at him, he could see she'd just dragged herself back to the here and now.

Soon, Arie was sitting in the chair by his side, and they began to partake of the delicious meal, with Arie plying him with questions about Italy. She was especially fascinated with the cuisine. Rome was no expert, but he did his best to satisfy her curiosity.

"So, what's your favorite Italian dish?" she asked, as she popped a bit of food into her mouth. "That's easy. Spaghetti."

"Spaghetti?" She laughed, and it was a lighthearted laugh that told him she was back to her perky mood. "That's so ordinary."

He shrugged. "That's why I like it. No fanfare, just hearty food." He reached for his glass of water and took a sip. "In fact, if you asked my brothers, I'd bet they'd say the same thing. When we were kids, we would eat it every day if they'd let us."

That made her tilt her head as she gazed at him, the light of curiosity shining in her eyes. "Are you from a big family?" He nodded. "Pretty big, I guess. I have three brothers and two sisters. That makes six of us, plus Mama and Papa, Nonno and Nonna and tons of aunts, uncles and cousins."

Arie rested her chin on her palm, her gaze never wavering from his face. "That's a huge family. What's a nono?"

"Nonno," Rome said, with a soft chuckle. "That's my grandpa. He's the one who always takes charge of fixing Christmas dinner. This year will be no exception."

Arie's eyes widened. "Your grandpa's still alive?"

Rome laughed. "Alive and well and strong as an ox. He'll be busy in the kitchen with Nonna by his side. I can promise you that."

"Wow." It was a soft, breathy whisper that was full of wonder. "It must be something, having all of you together. That's three generations." She shook her head. "No, four if there are any little ones in the picture."

He nodded. "My sisters have five kids between them, so it's quite a zoo when we all meet for the holidays."

She grinned. "I'd love to be a fly on that wall. It's got to be better than watching T.V."

That comment made Rome's smile fade. As he watched her face, his mood grew serious. "And is that what you do, Arie? Watch T.V when the holidays come around?"

For a second, her smile faltered, and then it disappeared altogether. She dropped her gaze then began toying with her fork. "Not always. Thanksgiving is usually busy, but Lena insists that we close for Christmas Day." She looked up, and as she spoke, her voice grew stronger. "I usually try to get out of the house. I help out at the soup kitchen downtown, but last year all the volunteer spots were taken, so I ended up staying home." She shrugged. "There was nothing else to do but watch T.V."

"And what about friends?"

"I go to Lena's sometimes, but I don't want to be a burden." She gave him a half-guilty look. "Sometimes, I make up stories, so she won't feel bad. Christmas is a time for family, you know. I don't want to spoil that for her all the time."

Rome stared at her for a second, sensing the loneliness she must be feeling. "Somehow," he said softly, "I don't think you would."

Then, filled with the sudden desire to comfort her, he slid his hand across the table and covered hers in what he hoped was a reassuring grasp.

At his touch, she looked up and her eyes shimmered with what could only be unshed tears.

That was his undoing. The sight of her sadness ripped into his soul. He reached out and took her other hand then got up, taking her with him. "Come to me, darling," he said quietly. "I need a hug."

When he saw her lips tremble, and when she stepped into his arms and clung to him like she would never let go, he knew he'd done the right thing. More than anything, what Arie needed right then was someone to hold on to, someone to show her that she mattered.

For a long time, Rome held her close, rocking her like a baby, wanting so badly to shield her from the pain. There was little he could do about the past but maybe, even for this one evening, he could make her forget her sorrow and live for the moment that they were together.

Placing a finger under her chin, he gently lifted her face to his, then gave her a feather-light kiss that told her she was special.

"Come," he said softly. "Let's dance."

ARIE COULD NOT BELIEVE what was happening. Just because Rome told her about his family, she'd almost turned into a blubbering mess. It had taken all of her self-control to keep the sobs inside and just hold on to him until the tumultuous waves of emotions subsided. It took a while but thankfully, by the time he asked her to dance, she was composed enough to take his hand and then lead him to her favorite part of the house.

It was a sitting room of sorts, with walls lined with books and a comfy sofa where she would often curl up with a good book. It was here that she had her music library, and it was here that she would often daydream about love and laughter and family. Will I ever get married, she would wonder, and have a husband to come home to me every evening, little ones running under foot, a doggy to bark and keep me up at night, and a fluffy old cat to warm my toes? But tonight, for the first time, she would not be alone, daydreaming in this room. Tonight, she would be dancing with Rome. And it was like a princess's dream come true. Like a fairy-tale prince, he led her onto the dance floor – in this case, the rug-covered floor of the sitting room – and, with the poise of a seasoned dancer, he led her through one old school love ballad then another, now dancing to Brian McKnight's 'Crazy Love' then Celine Dion's 'Because You Loved Me' then 'All My Life' by K-Ci & JoJo. By the time they got to 'Here and Now' by Luther Vandross, Arie was practically melting in Rome's arms.

And when he lowered his head to touch his lips to her bare shoulder, she was ready for anything he had to give. And, it seemed, he wanted to give plenty.

ROME FOR THE HOLIDAYS

Rome skimmed his lips over her super-sensitive skin, sending shivers up and down her body, making her bite her lip to keep from moaning. Then, just as she was recovering from that shock, he stepped up his attack, trailing kisses across her collarbone and up the column of her neck, making her gasp out loud.

Rome must have taken her audible reaction as license to take control, because he took that trail of kisses across her cheek until he'd covered her mouth with hi,s and was kissing her so ardently that sitting room, music, everything was forgotten in the heat of the passion between them.

When he finally released her lips, it was to bend and lift her into his arms, then he was striding over to the couch, where he laid her gently against the cushions.

As he sat on the edge of the sofa, gazing down at her with eyes dark with desire, Arie could see that he was just as affected as she was. Eyes hooded, his breathing shallow, the pulse beating at his throat was now visible, ample evidence of the height of his arousal.

And then, as she watched his face, she saw that there was something more. He wanted her, that much was obvious, but there was a kindness in his eyes, a hint of caring that she'd never seen before. And that, more than anything, made her want him more.

Reaching up, she pulled his face down to her, and this time, it was she who was taking the lead. Arie molded his lips to hers, and then she was kissing him so fiercely, he would have no doubt that she wanted him with every inch of her being. In that kiss, she put all the attraction she felt for him, all the pent-up desire, all the frustration of knowing he was so far removed from her, all the unrequited love that consumed her.

Rome answered in kind, and soon he was holding her to the promise she'd made in her kiss. Pressing her back into the cushions, he drew his mouth away to caress her neck, and then the tops of her breasts, with his mouth. He must have seen her nipples peak in her dress because, to her sweet relief, he slid the strap off her shoulders then down the length of her arms until her lace-covered breasts were exposed to his gaze. Without hesitation, he covered those sensitive orbs with sweet kisses that made her grow moist with desire.

She was ready for Rome in so many ways. Her body was eager, and so was she. Her mind, her soul, her heart, they were all attuned to the symphony he was playing with his lips and with his hands.

When Rome reached behind to unsnap her bra, she did not resist. Instead, she reached up to quickly loosen the buttons on his shirt, leaving his body bare to her hungry gaze. She was not disappointed. His body was painfully beautiful, so perfectly sculpted, she could find no flaw on him. Reaching up, she pulled him down, so she could feather kisses across his belly, then delicately lick the shallow dip of his navel, making him groan.

Spurred on by the sexy sound of his arousal, Arie reached for his belt buckle, her fingers shaking as she struggled to undo that one thing that was keeping her from enjoying all of him. When his hand slid down to cover hers, she sighed, glad that he would help her reach her goal.

But then, he released her hands and stepped back and away from the couch. To her surprise, instead of undoing the buckle,

Rome his shirt closed and swiftly buttoned it up again, hiding his beautiful, bare body from her gaze. His eyes never leaving hers, he tucked the shirt back into his trousers.

What in the world was going on?

Even as the confusion swept through her, Rome leaned over to pull her dress back up and over her exposed bosom. Then, he sat on the edge of the sofa and looked down at her. Slowly, he shook his head. "No," he said, his face serious. "We don't want this."

Arie could only stare up at him, searching his face for a clue to what she'd done wrong. "I don't understand. I thought...you wanted this, too."

"No, I don't," he said, his face rigid and his voice firm. "And neither do you."

He got up from the sofa where she lay, frozen and frigid like a statue made of marble.

"I'm going now," he said. "I'm sorry, but I just need to be alone. I have a lot to think about.

Arie just barely had the presence of mind to get up, straighten her clothes and walk him to the door. "I'll call you tomorrow," he said. "Goodnight, Arie."

Arie barely responded to the peck he placed on her forehead.

She just stood there, watching him walk back down the driveway, her heart weeping at the shock of his cold rejection.

CHAPTER SIX

B
ut he'd had to.

The fact was, it was right when they were about to cross that threshold, just at the point where, in another minute, they would be making love, that it hit him right between the eyes. He didn't want to make love to Arie just that day. He wanted her for always.

And just like that, Rome was in love.

It was the shock of that realization that had made him pull up short. It had been so sudden. He'd only known her little more than a month, but in his heart, he knew she was the one. Maybe it was her vulnerability; maybe it ws the way she had come to him, trusting him, not doubting his intentions. Immediately after that thought, another flashed through his mind. He didn't want their first time to be just casual sex. No, he wanted to do it right. Without that meaningful comitment, he could not go through with it.

But how could he have told Arie all that? He hadn't even had time to process it himself. He needed time to absorb the whole thing. Right then, he needed to be alone.

And so, he'd left – fled was probably a more accurate word – so that he could take stock of the new Rome Milano, the one who, for the first time in his life, was actually contemplating settling down.

ROME FOR THE HOLIDAYS

After two days of trying and not getting Arie, Rome had to fly out to Italy to be with his family for the holidays. It grieved him that he hadn't been able to kiss her goodbye. He hadn't even been able to speak to her. She was refusing all his calls.

Now, it was Christmas Eve, he was all the way in Italy and Arie, most likely, was all alone.

But Rome had another plan up his sleeve.

Christmas Day dawned sunny and bright in Italy. At least, that was what Rome heard. On that bright and beautiful morning, he was nowhere near the place. Instead, he was tearing up the wonderfully empty highway, on his way to Arie's house.

She'd refused his calls to her office. She'd refused to answer her cell phone. Today, he would try neither one. He would camp out on her doorstep, if he had to. The day would not end before he held Arie in his arms again.

As soon as he'd pulled up in front of her house, Rome hopped out of the Maserati and ran up the steps to pound on the front door. Remembering the bell, he pressed it two times, three times and four, and then he was pounding on the door again, anxious to see the woman who could make him feel whole.

He was just about to give up and implement that 'camping on the doorstep' last resort tactic he'd planned, when the door opened, and Arie came into view. For a fleeting second, he thought he saw something in her eyes. Was it joy? Relief? Could it be love? But then, .it disappeared, and although she smiled at him, it was a smile so tinged with hurt that all he wanted to do was gather her in his arms and protect her from all the pain she'd ever gone through.

Inwardly, he groaned. He was part of that pain, wasn't he? But now, he was here to set things right.

"Rome," she said, her voice soft and hesitant. "What are you doing here? I thought you'd be in Italy...with your family."

He shook his head. "I already saw them. I just got back last night. I couldn't stay away, Arie. I want to spend Christmas with you."

Eyes wide, she stared up at him, and then she shook her head. "With me? But why? I thought..." Her breath caught in her throat , and she bit her lip. Then she shook her head. "You said..." She broke off and her lips began to tremble.

Seeing her distress, Rome stepped forward and caught her hands in his. "I know what I said, honey, and I'm sorry I hurt you. So sorry." He lifted her hands to his lips and kissed them softly, then he looked deep into her eyes. "I left suddenly that night because something amazing happened. Something I just could not explain. I have to admit, it threw me upside down. I needed some time to work it out in my head."

He drew in his breath and now he was smiling down at her. She was listening intently and that was all he needed, just the chance to tell her how he felt. "Arie, that night we were together, I fell in love. It was like nothing I'd ever felt before." He took the chance and pulled her one step closer. "Arie, I'm in love with you. Will you make this Christmas the happiest I've ever had? Will you be my wife?"

Arie sucked in her breath and her grip on his hands tightened. "Rome," she gasped, "are you...do you...I...don't believe it."

"Believe it, my darling. I love you, and if you'll have me, you'll never spend another Christmas alone."

"But...we just met...like six weeks ago. Are you sure?" There was doubt in her gaze, but a light of hope was there, too.

She loved him. He could see it.

"I'm sure, Arie. One hundred percent. Call it love at first sight, call it a whirlwind romance. Call it whatever you want, as long as you say you'll be Mrs. Rome Milano. Will you say yes? Please?"

Arie shook her head, but she was laughing, her joy spilling out as she moved closer to press her face into his chest and wrap her arms around him. "Yes, Rome. Yes, yes, yes. I want to be your wife."

Rome was laughing, too, as he stroked her back and bent to kiss the top of her head. "Then let's go inside. This time, we're going to spend Christmas together."

And, he hoped, it would be the first of many, many Christmases together. And, if they were so blessed, one day there would be kids and grandkids to share it with.

And Arie, the newfound light in his life, would never be alone again.

CHAPTER SEVEN

It was a new couple that stepped off the front porch and walked into the house that day - a committed couple, one intending to spend the rest of their lives together.

Arie could not believe it. That couple, the one walking through those doors - she was a part of that pair She was, right then, holding hands with the man she loved, her soon-to-be husband.

She almost had to stop and pinch herself. Could this be her? If ever there was a dream come true, this was it.

And all those Christmases she'd spent all by herself, crying into her eggnog, like an ice cube in a hot oven, those memories were swiftly melting away, overwhelmed by the heat of the love emanating from two hearts on a high from the most potent potion there was – long and lasting love.

And it was at that thought, that she was suddenly hit by the ideal idea – what greater way to seal their love on this, her most consequential Christmas yet, than to give herself as a gift to Rome? On this, their first Christmas together, it would be a gift he would never forget.

And so, that settled in her mind, she tightened her grip on Rome's hand and began to pull him straight down the hallway, her primary purpose being to get him to the most private spot in this, her place of residence.

There, she planned to ravish her Rome, bathe his body with caresses and kisses, tickling and teasing him till he was so tormented, he would tear–

"Hey! Where are you dragging me off to?"

A tug at Arie's hand made her come to a sudden halt. More than that, it sent her fantasy flying.

With a fake frown meant to make her look mean, Ari turned around to glare at the man she was trying to kidnap. "Did I give you permission to speak?" she growled.

"Be a good little boy," she continued, warming to her new role as dominatrix." If you want to get your gift for Christmas, just keep quiet and come with me."

Rome blinked. And then, like the cutest little puppy, he tilted his head, his look first confused, then curious, then quickly turning to anticipation then ardor.

Rome licked his lips, then he set off, striding ahead, and this time it was he who was doing the tugging, pulling her along behind him, making Arie have to skip to keep up.

"Hey," she squeaked." Do you even know where you're going?"

Without slowing his pace, Rome kept on walking, forcing Arie into a fast trot behind him.

"It's got to be at the end of this hallway. But it doesn't matter. I just need you on a bed, ready to be ravished."

"Hey, where'd you get that idea? That I was ready to be ravished?"

"It's the Christmas gift you're gong to give me. You just made that clear. Don't back out now."

By this time, they were in the guest bedroom... not as good as her room, but it would do well enough.

And, by this time, Arie was past being coy. If it was a ravishing Rome wanted ,well, it was a ravishing Rome would get.

As he was pulling her toward the plush–pillowed bed in the middle of the room, Arie pulled back then pushed him in the direction of the ensuite. When she snapped the light on, he blinked. Taking advantage of his momentary confusion, she reached up to begin unbuttoning his shirt.

"Let's get you nice and clean," she whispered." I want a taste of that delicious body of yours."

Like he liked the sound of that, Rome made a soft moan, and then he was loosening the button even faster than she was.

As soon as the shirt flapped open, revealing his taut body, Arie pushed it off his shoulders and let it fall to the floor.

Next, she reached down to unbuckle his belt, but it was like Rome couldn't keep his calm long enough to wait for her. So great was his haste, that the next moment, he was batting her hand away and unbuckling his belt, deftly doing that thing that would bare his most private part to her view.

Suddenly shy, Arie stepped back, but it was a bit too late for shyness. No. Way too late.

Her eyes widened. What she was seeing was fabric stretched so taut that it seemed to be struggling to subdue a swollen snake.

Lord. Talk about deceptive. Who would have guessed that Rome, so lean and lithe, would be packing such punch?

But as Arie was backing away, Rome was rushing toward his goal of claiming her impulsively promised Christmas gift. Seconds after stepping back, wide-eyed, Arie's eyes were widening even more, unable to step away fro the sight before her.

There, solid and strong, and surrounded by jet-black strands that seemed like they were the softest setting and the perfect protection, stood that precious pole. It was now protruding from its previously private place, ihat place where it had been resting, relaxed, between Rome's legs.

Clearly, in its swollen state, it was now ready to reign supreme.

Arie sucked in her breath, but that was as far as she got, because Rome had stepped toward her and was now tackling the buttons of her blouse, apparently hoping to help her speed up the process of doing for her what she just had him do for himself. He was clearly determined to bare her body to his heated gaze.

Knowing there was now no turning back, Arie swallowed her sudden shyness and let Rome's gaze roam all over her near-naked body. Now, gone was the blouse, and then he was peeling her pants down her legs, leaving her standing in front of him in nothing but black lacy bra and panties to match, a pair that emphasized the length of her legs while the top featured the fullness of her breasts.

ROME FOR THE HOLIDAYS

Now, it was Rome's turn to stare. And stare, he did, his eyes widening in obvious wonder, his gaze glowing in obvious appreciation, his lips widening in a smile so sincere, yet so sexy, that Arie's legs trembled in anticipation.

It was Rome who finally broke the spell. "Come," he said calmly, sounding much calmer than she was feeling, "let's go take that shower we came here for."

Arie blinked. She'd forgotten about that. "Y...yes," she stammered. "Sure." Then, suddenly shy again, she turned her back to Rome, and reached behind to unclasp her bra and let her breasts fall free. Quickly, before she could change her mind, she hooked her thumb into the top of her underwear and bent to push the garment down her legs, down to the ground.

"Mmm". The soft moan that came from behind Arie was followed by a warm hand that began to softly stroke her bum, making her jump. It was then that she realized that, in turning her back to Rome and then bending over, she had given him an uncensored view of her bottom. No wonder he had come closer to claim her body by placing his palm on her posterior.

Knowing that if they didn't speed things up, they wouldn't even make it back to the bedroom, Arie quickly flung bra and panty to the floor and reached out to grab Rome's wrist. She dragged him toward the tub, turnng on the faucet even as she did.

Within seconds, they'd both stepped in and were standing beneath the wet, warm spray. Like they were both thinking the same thing, both eager to return to the bedroom, Rome grabbed her washcloth, poured flower bouquet scented bath gel onto it, and then he was soaping her body and then his, seeming set on completing the task in quick time. As they stood under the cleansing stream, there was no caressing, only a focus on finishing as fast as possible. Following the shower, they found time for one last thing. When Arie threw a spare toothbrush at Rome, he caught it deftly.

As soon as they'd finished brushing, he picked her up in arms so muscled and sttrong that she could hardly wait to have them wrapped around her.

For that wish, Arie did not have to wait long. Rome laid her on top of the big bed and climbed on beside her. Then, so quickly she was caught off guard, he claimed her lips in a kiss that left her breathless.

She'd hardly recovered from that kiss, when he slid is lips away, down her neck, down the mounds of her breasts, where he let his warm, wet tongue slide even further down, until those lips were hovering over her right nipple, turgid and tortured, hungering for release.

And then, so softly and sweetly, Rome lowered his lips to suck that puckered nipple into his mouth, making Arie moan in ecstasy.

It was such sweet release, with his lips sucking, his tongue stroking, his breath warming her skin. And then, thanks be, he turned his attention to the other turgid nipple, moving his masterful ministrations to that other breast, so swollen with want.

Sweet thrills sweeping her to heavenly heights, Arie moaned, her body writhing with want. And it was that want that made her reach out, and with a strength she didn't know she had, she hooked her hands under Rome's arms and hauled him up, over and over her body, his bare chest just above her face, and so it was that she was soon sucking on his nipple, making him do some moaning of his own.

The sexy sound making her bold, Arie released that nipple and, heaving him even further forward till his abs were just above her, she moved lower down his body, feathering quick kisses over his heated skin, moving lower and lower still, till she'd reached that rigid rod that jotted out from its forest of fine, jet black hair.arie

To her surprise, and maybe to Rome's as well, Arie turned bold. Thinking of nothing but the thrill of the moment, she opened her mouth and covered that beautiful bulb at the end of the now red and raging rod that rose from the hairy garden between Rod's legs.

Poor thing. It was clearly tormented. Arie had to put the sweet, sexy, suffering stick out of its misery.

With that in mind, she began to lather that head with lascivious licks from her tongue, tasting the mouthwatering maleness of Rome's manhood, her own mouth watering with each lick. And then she was sucking that sweet stick deep into her mouth, seeking to soothe with her sweet seduction, seeking to suck all the suffering, all the redness away.

Like his body was beginning to be the boss, Rome's hips began jerking, and soon he began booking forward, forcing his dick even deeper in her mouth, almost making her gag.

That was when Arie knew it was time. There was no way she was going to let this man, now no her man, spill his seed without having him first partake of the feast she'd prepared: her sweet spot, her most private place, her pretty little pussy [if she should say so herself].

Immediately, she jerked her head back, pulling away from his penis before it could explode.

"Oh, God. No." Rome's guttural groan did not stop Arie from going for her goal. Before he knew what she was doing, she'd wrapped her arms around his body and pulled him down onto her. As she pressed his chest against her soft breasts, she lifted her legs and wrapped them around his lean hips.

There was another groan from him, this one deeper than the first, as if he were in a state of true torment. "Arie," he groaned. "I can't hold back. My condom."

She gasped. That? Now? When they'd already committed to marriage? For her, there was no turning back now. Still, she tried to hold on. "Where?" she gasped, and clutched his shoulder as he squeezed his eyes shut and dipped his head.

She clutched him even tighter. God, please don't let him come now, not before –

She tightened her grip. "Where?"

"My trousers. Wallet."

Arie didn't wait for him to say anymore. With all her might, she pushed him up and off her, making him fall over onto his back. Then, she drove onto the floor to dig into his trouser pocket to get his wallet. In seconds, she was back on the bed, packet already between her teeth, ripping it open to reveal its precious contents.

Quick as a flash, Arie was rolling the sheath down Rome's sword, now rigid and rearing to go. Well, she was ready.

Taking charge, Arie climbed over Rome's body until she was straddling his hips. Then, with the determination of a damsel in distress [from want of sweet sex], she positioned her pussy over that precious pole, then sank down, down, until it was embedded deep inside her depths.

And then she began to ride, slowly at first, then picking up pace as she planted her palms on Rome's chest.

And so she rode, revelling in the way he threw his head back into the pillows, eyes shut tight, gasps escaping his lips, as his hips bucked, his rod thrusting deep inside her red – hot core.

And so they rode, sharing the sweetest of sensations as they ravished each other, panting out their pleasure, their bodies trembling from the titillation of the tantalizing thrills.

They were moving and moaning, melting like molasses into each other's arms, and then the momentous moment came, amplifying their moans, making them meld into one ultimate utterance of unparallelled pleasure.

As one, the air rushed out of them, each one lost in their own tumultuous tornado, a storm of epic proportion's that swept each one up, sending them swirling in a cyclone of sensation.

And then, the burgeoning bubble burst, and with a whoosh, Rome collapsed on top of his partner in this, their temporary paradise.

It was several seconds of heaving chests and gasping breaths before Arie and Rome were finally able to catch their breaths.

With a sigh, Rome rolled away, to collapse onto his back, on the bed beside her.

With a soft sigh, and a smile on her lips, Arie reached out to stroke the face of the beautiful man by her side, her man, the one who would forevermore be a part of her life.

"That was your gift, my love," she breathed, as she stroked. "The gift of me. Merry Christmas."

But soon, her strokes stilled.

They were stilled when Rome reached up to take her hand in his. Then, he took that hand and gently pressed her palm to his lips.

"Thank you, my love," he said softly, his voice a deep rumble. "That was a Christmas gift I hope I'll be getting all the days of my life."

At his words, Arie's his heart melted. It was a wish she planned to fulfil for as long as they both should live.

Arie was so happy, she let out a soft sigh. This was her happiest Christmas, ever. "Thank you for coming back to be with me for the holidays."

Rome reached out to pull her close, his arms creating for her, a warm and welcoming cocoon.

"You've got it wrong, my sweet. I don't plan to be here only for the holidays. I plan to be with you for always."

Her heart swelling with love, she rested her cheek on Rome's chest.

Now, if that wasn't the best Christmas gift, Arie didn't know what was.

.

Thank you for reading!
I hope you had fun reading this story. For more information
on my novels, please visit my blog for updates.

http://www.judyangelo.blogspot.com/

If you wish to drop me a line, please send your e-mail to:
judyangeloauthor@gmail.com
I would love to hear from you!

Sneak Preview

Rome for Always

(Sequel to 'Rome for the Holidays')

ROME FOR THE HOLIDAYS

.. ⚬ ..

CHAPTER ONE

I

Arie could not believe what she'd done. Seriously, what kind of fool had she been, to think this would work? A marriage proposal from super-handsome billionaire, Rome Milano? She'd been over the moon. But now, one month into their engagement, she was having second thoughts.

And, unfortunately, it was for good reason because when Rome found out she'd kept something so serious from him, she didn't know if he would ever forgive her.

She shook her head, trying desperately to clear her mind of the thought that was both depressing and exciting at the same time. Goodness, she felt like she was being torn in two. With a hiss of frustration, she hopped up off the concrete bench and pulled her jacket closer around her. She'd had enough of gazing into the waters of her backyard pond. If she sat there one minute longer, she would go mad.

She was heading back toward the house when her cell phone rang. She dug it out of her pocket and glanced at the screen. Lena. Arie almost sighed. She wasn't in the mood for a chat, but when her business partner called, she knew she had better answer. This could be important.

"Hey, Lena. What's up?" She forced a note of cheerfulness into her voice, even though she was feeling anything but. "Hey, girl," Lena said, sounding cheery enough for both of them. "What are you doing on this beautiful Sunday morning?"

Arie grimaced. As she'd told herself earlier, she wasn't in the mood for chit-chat. Apparently, Lena was. Still, this was her long-time partner and friend. She had to at least try.

"Oh, nothing," she said. "I'll probably just catch up on my reading."

"What? On a lovely day like this?" Lena sounded appalled. "I thought for sure you and Rome would be doing something special. Or is he away? Off to Italy, is he?"

"No, he's in Sydney right now. Remember I told you about the launch of his men's formal wear line?"

"Oh, yeah. I forgot it was this weekend." Lena clucked her tongue. "Now, don't you be sitting there, moping around the house, missing him. Do you want me to come over?"

"No, it's okay." Arie was quick to respond. The last thing she needed was to have to put on a happy face when all she wanted to do was cry. "I'll be all right. I'll call him later. He'll be back in a few days, anyway."

"Well, all right. If you're sure." Lena sounded doubtful, almost like she could sense that all was not well on the other end of the line. "I'll give you a buzz later, okay?"

"Okay," Arie said meekly, knowing that her friend would do as she'd promised, no matter what reassurance she tried to give her. No-nonsense and stubborn, that was Lena.

Arie did spend the rest of the morning moping around the house, the very thing Lena had warned her not to do. And she was missing Rome. Terribly. But, on top of all that, she was consumed with guilt for what she'd done, and for what she was about to do.

To read more about Arie and Rome, get your copy of 'Rome for Always' from your favorite online retailer.

THE BILLIONAIRE BROTHERHOOD

THE BILLIONAIRE BROTHERS KENT

THE CASTILLOS

HOLIDAY EDITIONS

Rome for the Holidays (Novella)
Rome for Always (Novel)

The NAUGHTY AND NICE Series

Volume 1 - **Naughty by Nature**

COMEDY, CONFLICT & ROMANCE Series

THE BILLIONAIRE
BACHELORETTES OF BEL-AIR

Book 1 -In Bed with the Enemy

NOVELLAS

The Billionaire's Bold Bet
Tamed by the Billionaire - The Sequel

COLLABORATIONS

A is for Arrangement – Eden Adams

INTERNATIONAL

SPA - Domado por el Multimillionario
FRE - La Milliardaire Apprivoisee
SPA - Romance de la Criada en los EU
FRE - En Amour avec la Femme de Chambre
GER - Vom Milliardar Gezahmt
SPA - La Novia Cautiva del Multimillionario
SPA - Engano Peligroso
JAP - For titles in Japanese, contact Tuttle Mori
Agency, Tokyo

NONFICTION

How to Write a Romance Novel

COLLECTIONS

THE BILLIONAIRE BROTHERHOOD, Coll. I - Vols. 1 - 4

THE BILLIONAIRE BROTHERHOOD, Coll. II - Vols. 5 - 8

THE BILLIONAIRE BROTHERHOOD, Coll. III - Vols. 9 - 12

BILLIONAIRE BROS. KENT - Books 1 - 4

THE BILLIONAIRE BROTHERHOOD DOUBLE COLLECTION - Vols. 1 - 8

THE BILLIONAIRE BROTHERHOOD MEGA-COLLECTION - Vols. 1 - 12

THE BILLIONAIRE BROTHERS KENT - Vols. 1 - 4

THE CASTILLOS - Vols. 1 - 4

COMEDY, CONFLICT & ROMANCE - Vols. 1 - 3

HOME for the HOLIDAYS - Vols. 1 - 3

• • ⚜ • •

Author contact:

JUDY ANGELO

judyangeloauthor@gmail.com

ROME FOR THE HOLIDAYS

Copyright © 2016 Judy Angelo
Phoenix Publishing Limited

This book is a work of fiction. The names, characters, places, and incidents are products of the writer's imagination or have been used fictitiously. Any resemblance to persons, living or dead, is entirely coincidental.

• • ⚬◦⚬ • •

Author contact:
judyangeloauthor@gmail.com

Cover Artist: Ramona Lockwood (Covers by Ramona)

Don't miss out!

Visit the website below and you can sign up to receive emails whenever JUDY ANGELO publishes a new book. There's no charge and no obligation.

https://books2read.com/r/B-A-WPD-LBYB

BOOKS 2 READ

Connecting independent readers to independent writers.

Did you love *Rome for the Holidays*? Then you should read *Rome for Always*[1] by JUDY ANGELO!

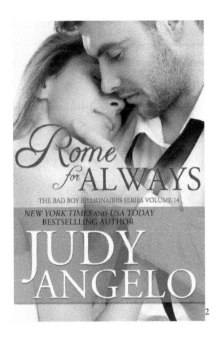

NEW YORK TIMES & USA TODAY best-selling author, Judy Angelo, presents:

ROME FOR ALWAYS Sequel to the novella, Rome for the Holidays, in the collection, 'Hot, Sexy & Bad'

SHE HAD ROME FOR THE HOLIDAYS, BUT WILL SHE HAVE HIM FOR ALWAYS?

Arie Angelis is on top of the world. She's engaged to the man of her dreams, the super-handsome and successful CEO of Belitalia, Rome Milano. She could not believe it when he

---

1. https://books2read.com/u/bOrvoA

2. https://books2read.com/u/bOrvoA

proposed on Christmas Day. Of course, she said yes! But then, only a month into their engagement there's a turn of events that threatens to steal her newfound happiness. In the past she'd made a life-altering choice. Now it's time to stand by that decision. The only question is, will Rome stand with her or will it send him running?

Rome Milano knows a good thing when he sees it and when he meets Arie he has no doubt that she's the one for him. He falls so swiftly in love with her that within weeks of meeting her he's proposing. He can't be any happier when she accepts. But there's just one problem - how to convince the important people in his life that this is for real. Now that he's found happiness will he be forced to choose between love and loyalty?

It's decision time on both sides. Through it all, will love prevail?

Read more at judyangelo.blogspot.com.

Also by JUDY ANGELO

Bad Boy Billionaires - Where Are They Now?
Tamed by the Billionaire - The Sequel

Billionaire Bachelorettes of Bel-Air
In Bed with the Enemy

Billionaire Brotherhood
The Billionaire Brotherhood III, Vols. 9 - 12

Historias Multimillionarias para Navidad
Rome para Navidad

KNOWLEDGE in a NUTSHELL
How to Write a Romance Novel

MADE FOR THE MOVIES Fantasy Romance
Trading Spaces
Back from the Future
Back from the Future with BONUS Trading Spaces

Multimillonarios Machos
Domada por el Multimillionario
Domado por el Multimillionario, Bilingual Version

The BAD BOY BILLIONAIRES Series
To Tame a Tycoon
Sweet Seduction
Daddy by December
To Catch a Man (in 30 Days or Less)
Bedding Her Billionaire Boss
Her Indecent Proposal
So Much Trouble When She Walked In
Married by Midnight
Bad Boy Billionaires - Collection II, Vols. 5 - 8
Bad Boy Billionaires Mega-Collection Vols 1 - 12

THE BILLIONAIRE BROTHERHOOD
Tamed by the Billionaire (Roman's Story)
Maid in the USA (Pierce's Story)

The Comedy, Conflict and Romance Series
Taming the Fury
Outwitting the Wolf
Romancing Malone
Comedy, Confict & Romance - The Collection

The Naughty and Nice Series
Naughty by Nature

Standalone
The Billionaire's Bold Bet

Watch for more at judyangelo.blogspot.com.

About the Author

New York Times & USA Today best-selling author, Judy Angelo, considers herself a 'traveling writer'. She currently resides in Ontario, Canada but prior to that she called New York and then Illinois home. She has also spent considerable time in the Caribbean, Latin America and Europe. She loves to travel as it provides her with interesting and diverse settings for her stories.

Judy fell in love with romance novels as a teenager and has never lost her passion for these stories of love and life, conflict and reconciliation, relationships and family. For her, it was a natural progression from reading romance novels to writing them. So far, she has written over 70 romance novels, including the best-selling Bad Boy Billionaires series. Her other series include The Billionaire Brothers Kent, The Castillos, and the Comedy, Conflict & Romance series.

She hopes to continue entertaining her readers with intriguing stories for many years to come.

Website - www.judyangelo.blogspot.com

I would love to hear from you! judyangeloauthor@gmail.com

Read more at judyangelo.blogspot.com.

Lightning Source UK Ltd.
Milton Keynes UK
UKHW011035070223
416609UK00008B/2201

Talk about sexy as sin...

Arie Angelis is floored when she lays eyes on the handsome hunk seated at the head table at the holiday event she's catering. She literally can't take her eyes off him. She's always prided herself on being the consummate professional, but not this time. But, attracted or not, when she finds out who he is she realizes he's way out of her reach. But you can't stop a girl from dreaming...

Rome Milano is used to getting what he wants but when he meets the hot and heavenly Arie Angelis he learns that he can't always have his way. He's used to calling the shots but, if the lady has her way, not this time...

New York Times & USA Today best-selling author, Judy Angelo considers herself a 'traveling writer'. She currently resides in Ontario, Canada but prior to that she called New York and then Illinois home. She has also spent considerable time in the Caribbean, Latin America and Europe. She loves to travel, as it provides her with interesting and diverse settings for her stories.

www.judyangelo.blogspot.com

judyangeloauthor@gmail.com

ISBN 979-8-201-90150-9